SERGIO
SEES THE
GOOD

This book is dedicated to my
parents, John and Barbara Ryden,
who always taught me to notice
the little good things in life.

—L.R

SERGIO
SEES THE
GOOD

A Story of One Not So Bad Day

WRITTEN BY **LINDA RYDEN**

ILLUSTRATED BY **SHEARRY MALONE**

TILBURY HOUSE PUBLISHERS, THOMASTON, MAINE

Sergio came home from school and slammed the door. "What's wrong?" said his mother. "How was your day?"

"Terrible! It was a terrible day." said Sergio.
"I dropped my lunch tray and my food went everywhere!"

He threw his backpack onto the floor. "It was a completely awful day."

"Are you sure the whole day was terrible?" his mom asked. "Why don't we make sure?"

"Huh?" said Sergio "How?"

"Go get the scale from the high shelf. You know, the old one that belonged to your grandfather."

"What for?" asked Sergio.

"You'll see. And bring me that jar full of marbles from your room," said Mom mysteriously.

"Okay . . ." said Sergio, feeling really confused.

"So," said Mom. "Let's rewind your day. We'll go back to the beginning and try to remember everything that happened."

"What are the scale and marbles for?" asked Sergio.

"The right side of the scale is going to be the good side and the left side is going to be the bad side. For every bad thing you remember from today, we'll put a marble on the bad side, and for every good thing you remember, we'll put a marble on the good side. When we're done, we'll see which one is heavier. That's how we'll decide if it was a good or bad day."

"Okay," said Sergio, "but I already know that the bad side is going to be way heavier."

"Let's just wait and see, okay?" Mom said.

"Well, I told you about one really bad thing that happened when I dropped my lunch. It ruined the whole day."

"Yes, I think you could put in three marbles for that," said Mom.

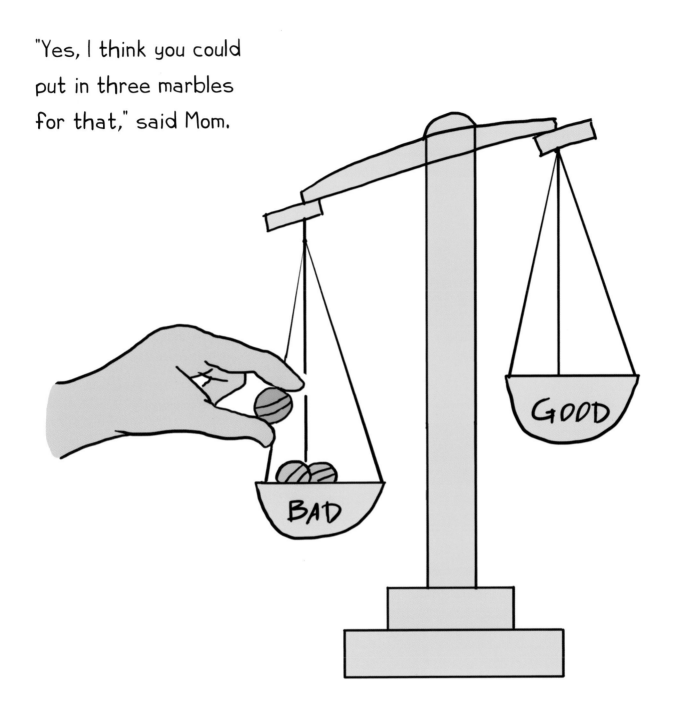

Sergio put three marbles into the bad side. The scale tipped all the way to the left. "Yup, that's what my day was like. Totally bad."

"Now," said Mom, "let's get started with the rewind. What's the first thing that happened today?"

"Well, I woke up," said Sergio.

"In your nice warm bed?"

"Uh, yeah . . . ."

"So put one marble in the good side. Not everybody is lucky enough to have a warm bed to wake up in."

"Okay," said Sergio.

"Then what?" asked Mom.

"Uh, I had breakfast: waffles, my second favorite breakfast food."

"Well, that's good. Marble please," said Mom, gesturing toward the scale. Sergio put another marble in the good side.

"Then I played basketball with Henry before school and made a three-pointer!"

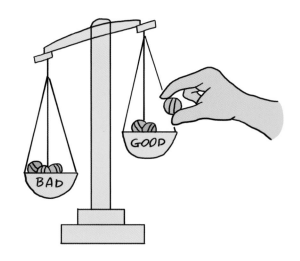

"Mmm-hmm," said Mom, smiling.

"I know. Marble please," said Sergio, smiling just a little.

"But then some older kids came over and took the basketball," he said. "That was definitely not good."

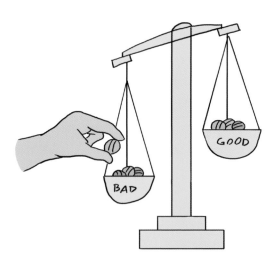

"Okay, then put another marble in the bad side," said Mom. "Then what happened?"

MATH
TEST

POSTPONED

8 ÷ 124   6 × 36
12 × 3   4 ÷ 84

"We were supposed to have a math test, but it was postponed. That's definitely good." Sergio dropped another marble in the good side.

"And next?"

BAD   GOOD

"That's when the whole day was ruined," said Sergio. "I was walking over to the lunch table and I dropped my tray. It was a huge mess. Peas went rolling everywhere, and kids laughed at me."

"Oh dear . . . ."

"It was so embarrassing."

"You could put an extra marble in the bad side for getting laughed at," said Mom.

"So then what happened," asked Mom. "Did you clean it up by yourself?"

"Well, no. Henry and Yoab and Tyaja helped me clean it up, and then Mr. Howell the custodian came over with the big broom. He wasn't mad at all! He's really nice."

"So where does the next marble go?"

"Good side, I guess," said Sergio. "People were pretty nice to me."

"But you didn't have any lunch," said Mom. "That's bad." She reached over to put a marble in the bad side, but Sergio stopped her.

"Actually, Henry gave me his apple, Yoab gave me half his sandwich, and Tyaja gave me her cookie."

"Sounds like a pretty good lunch. And pretty good friends!" said Mom.

"I know, I know," said Sergio. "Another marble on the good side!"

"Then what?"

"In the afternoon we had music class
and Mr. Holmes let us make up songs.

"Yoab and I wrote a song about the peas that fell on the floor. It's called 'Peas on Earth.' Want to hear it?"

"Maybe later," said Mom. "Marble, please . . . ."

"Oh, and I walked home with Tyaja and she told me a funny joke."

Sergio put another marble in the good side, then said, "Hey, all this remembering is making me hungry. What's for dinner?"

"Your dad made macaroni and cheese," said Mom.

"My favorite!!! I guess I'd better put in another marble."

"Well look at that," said Mom. "The good side of the scale is pretty heavy. Do you still think this was a totally bad day?"

"Gee, I guess not. It was actually pretty great! How come I was so focused on that one bad thing?"

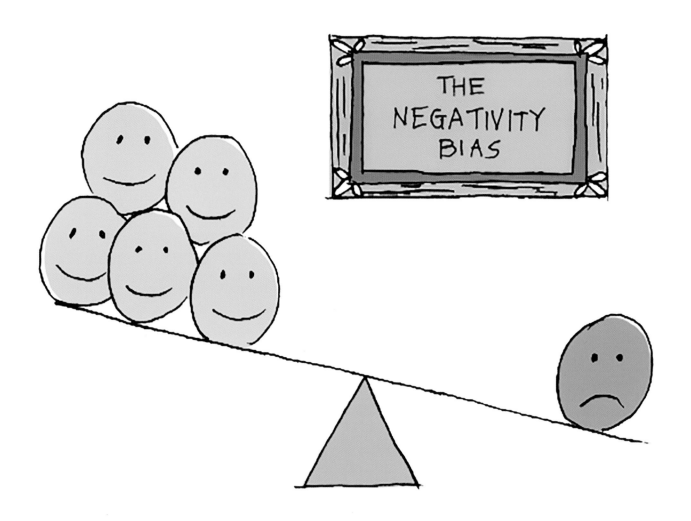

"That's just the way our brains work," said Mom. "They're wired to keep us safe, and they make sure we remember dangerous things. Scientists call this the negativity bias: Our brains focus on and remember negative things and let good things slide right out."

"Why?" asked Sergio.

"Well, this bias probably helped our early ancestors, who were mostly focused on trying not to be eaten by big animals! It's not as helpful today."

"But doesn't it still help? I mean, remember when I touched that cactus and it really hurt? I'll never do that again! Thank you, negativity bias!"

"Yup, that's what the negativity bias is for. But sometimes it can make us think that life isn't as great as it really is. We forget about all the little good things that happen and just focus on bad stuff."

"Yeah, that's definitely what happened to me."

"The neat thing is that noticing and being thankful for the little good things is a great way to overcome the negativity bias and see our lives more clearly. We don't have to pretend that bad things don't happen, but remembering positive things helps to keep the scales a little more balanced."

"Cool." said Sergio.

"I'm going to go warm up that mac and cheese," said Mom, and she headed into the kitchen.

Sergio looked at Phoebe and said, "I think I better put in one more marble." He dropped a marble in the good side and whispered, "Thanks, Mom!"

PUTTING THE NEGATIVITY BIAS IN ITS PLACE

I've been teaching mindfulness to students at Lafayette Elementary School in Washington, DC since 2003. I wrote *Sergio Sees the Good* to help children and their families understand the negativity bias and learn how it can be kept in perspective by practicing gratitude.

The negativity bias is our tendency to focus on and remember painful, embarrassing, or threatening experiences more than positive ones. When Sergio was pricked by a cactus, his brain filed that memory in a "Don't Forget This" drawer to prevent him from touching a cactus again. The negativity bias is helpful that way; it protects us from danger. But have you ever focused so much on a negative experience—perhaps a minor humiliation like spilling your lunch tray as Sergio did—that you've been unable to enjoy the good things going on around you for the rest of the day? If you have (and who hasn't?), you know all about the negativity bias.

Unless we're in immediate danger, it's healthier to focus on the positive things in our lives—healthier, but often harder. We remember the good big things like a great trip or a special event, but we tend to forget about the good little things that happen every day. Taking time to notice and appreciate good things allows our brains to capture those memories and file them in a long-term storage drawer right next to the bad memories. The result is that we see our lives more positively—and more realistically.

Here are three practices that help:

How Does the Scale Balance?

When you feel you are having a bad day, you might try the scale-and-marbles exercise that Sergio's mom helped him do. If you don't have a balance scale, use two dishes or cups, labeling one "Good" and the other "Bad." If you don't have marbles, use candies, dried peas, or uncooked macaroni. Any same-sized small objects will do. This is a lovely exercise to do with a partner who can help you see the small positive things you might otherwise overlook.

Make a Gratitude Journal

Developing a regular gratitude practice is great for your peace of mind, and it's easy: simply carve out a little time to write and draw about things you are grateful for.   Recording these feelings of gratitude will help you balance the impact of the negativity bias. To start this simple practice:

1. *Choose a notebook to serve as your gratitude journal.*

2. *Choose a consistent time to write in it each day or week.*

3. *Write or draw at least one thing you are grateful for each time.*

4. *Periodically read what you have written, especially when you are having a bad day.*

5. *If you like, share your journal with a friend or family member.*

Keeping a gratitude journal can be a powerful classroom or family activity, especially when people are willing to share what they have written.

A Gratitude Mindfulness Practice
And here is a meditation that helps us focus on the positive:

1. *Find a comfortable seat and close your eyes.*

2. *Think of four people whom you love or care deeply about. Imagine their faces smiling at you. Feel what that feels like.*

3. *The next time you breathe in, silently say thank you to these people.*

4. *When you breathe out, think about how you love and care for these people.*

5. *Do this for a few more breaths: when you breathe in, say thank you. When you breathe out, think about how much you love and care for these people.*

6. *Take two more deep breaths and open your eyes.*

You can use this same exercise to thank and appreciate coaches, teachers, friends, pets, nature, the world, and anything else you are grateful for.

I hope these practices are helpful to you and those you care about. For more information about the negativity bias, visit the Greater Good Science Center website at *https://greatergood.berkeley. edu*. My Peace of Mind website provides additional articles and video links at *https://teachpeaceof-mind.org/Resources*.

—Linda Ryden

Tilbury House Publishers
12 Starr Street
Thomaston, Maine 04861
800-582-1899 • www.tilburyhouse.com

Text © 2019 by Peace of Mind
Illustrations © 2019 by Shearry Malone

Hardcover ISBN 978-0-88448-731-9
eBook ISBN 978-0-88448-733-3

First hardcover printing February 2019

15 16 17 18 19 20 XXX 10 9 8 7 6 5 4 3 2 1

Library of Congress Control Number: 2018959953

Designed by Frame25 Productions
Printed in Korea by Artin Printing Co.
October 2018
82837

LINDA RYDEN is the full-time Peace Teacher at Lafayette Elementary School, a public school in Washington, DC, where she teaches weekly 45-minute classes to more than 600 children. She is also the creator of the Peace of Mind program and curriculum series, which includes *Peace of Mind: Core Curriculum for Grades 1 and 2* and *Peace of Mind: Core Curriculum for Grades 3-5*. Her work has been recognized in the *Washington Post* and the *Huffington Post*, and her program has been featured on local CBS, ABC and Fox5 news stations. Linda's books include *Rosie's Brain*, which uses a humorous story to introduce elementary school students to mindfulness skills. She is also the author of *Henry Is Kind* and the forthcoming *Tyaja Uses the Think Test*. Linda lives in Washington, DC with her husband, their two children, and their dog Phoebe.

SHEARRY MALONE studied art at Lipscomb University in Nashville. She is the illustrator of the *Absolutely Alfie* books, a spinoff from the *EllRay Jakes* series. In *Henry Is Kind* and *Sergio Sees the Good*, Shearry's loose, quirky illustrations make Henry, Sergio, and their pals as universally appealing as the kids in Charlie Brown's world.